Fantastic Feats

by David Orme

Trailblazers

Fantastic Feats: Don't Try This At Home
by David Orme
Educational consultant: Helen Bird

Illustrated by Martin Bolchover

Published by Ransom Publishing Ltd.
Radley House, 8 St. Cross Road, Winchester, Hampshire SO23 9HX
www.ransom.co.uk

ISBN   978 1 84167 652 4

First published in 2008
Reprinted 2009, 2014

Illustrations copyright © 2008 Martin Bolchover
'Get the Facts' section - images copyright: U.S. Air Force/Ashely Silvey; Jan Rihak; Marc Summers; Brian Sullivan; Aidan Jones; Giorgio Brugnoni; Patrick Herrera; Ransom Publishing.

Every effort has been made to locate all copyright holders of material used in this book. If any errors or omissions have occurred, corrections will be made in future editions of this book.

A CIP catalogue record of this book is available from the British Library.

Fantastic Feats

Contents

Why are these
hot dogs here?

DON'T TRY THIS AT HOME!

Fantastic Feats

Get the facts

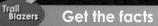

Amazing feats

Do you enjoy a challenge?

- or do you say

I can't do that!

COULD YOU ...

- Climb mount Everest?
- Eat 8 kilos of cow's brains in fifteen minutes?
- Jump through fire?

The famous tight rope walker **Blondin** achieved one of the greatest feats of all time. In 1859 he crossed the **Niagara falls** on a tight rope.

Blondin!

Then he did it again – on a **bicycle**!

And again – carrying someone on his back!

Cup of tea anyone?

Once he stopped in the middle – to cook his **breakfast!**

DON'T TRY THIS AT HOME!

How tough are you?

What do you have to do to become ...

THE WORLD'S STRONGEST PERSON?

? Carry a huge rock called a Husafell stone. *(Don't drop it on your feet ...)*

? Lift a car. *(This is called the deadlift.)*

Walk carrying heavy weights?
(This is called the farmer's walk.)

DON'T TRY THIS... oh you know where

Pull a truck 100 metres along the road.
(Hope they've taken the brakes off!)

Mr Memory

Look at the pictures
below for 30 seconds.

**Now
cover them
with your hands.**

How many things can
you remember?

Now look at the numbers below for **30 seconds**.

Then close the book and see how many you can remember – in the right order!

```
3.14159265358979323846264338327950
2884197169399375105820974944592
307164062862089986280348253421170
6794428810975665933446128475648233
7867831652712019091456485566923460
3486104543266482133936072602491412
73724587006606315588174881520920
```

TOUGH, EH?

But not for Mr **Akira Haraguchi**, of Japan.

Mr Haraguchi remembered these 300 numbers, **plus 83,131 more!**

Half way through reading them out, he forgot where he was – so he started again!

Umm...

Do you think Mr Haraguchi ever forgets his phone number?

Climbing Mount Everest

This is the **ultimate challenge**.

Many people have died trying to climb this mountain. A total of 19 people died in the year 1996.

You can get trapped or lost because of bad weather.

The top four thousand feet is called the **Death Zone**. There isn't enough oxygen in the air. Without extra oxygen, your body will collapse after a few days.

There is no one there to rescue you if you are in trouble.

On May 15th, 2005, **Mark Inglis** made it to the top of Everest.

SO WHAT?

In 1982 Mark had been climbing in New Zealand.

He was trapped in an ice cave.

When he was rescued, he had frost-bite in his legs. Both legs were **amputated** (cut off) below the knee.

That didn't stop him tackling the World's greatest challenge.

THAT'S WHAT!

DEATH ZONE

Not so amazing?

Some feats look absolutely amazing.

How would you like to **walk on fire**?

Or lie on a **bed of nails** and let someone put a **block** on your **stomach** and **smash it** with a **hammer**?

How do they do it?

Firewalking

The ash from the burning charcoal or wood stops the worst of the heat reaching your feet.

If you walk across quickly, the soles of your feet will help insulate you. Water or sweat on your feet can protect you.

But: the fire has to be just right for it to work – so **leave it to the experts!**

> Wow! Amazing feet!

DON'T TRY THIS AT HOME!

Why don't the nails hurt?
Because there are lots of them.

Bed of Nails

If you sit on one nail, the whole weight of your body will press down on it. **Ow!**

If you lie on **hundreds of nails**, each one only has to carry a little bit of you. This isn't enough to break your skin.

The **hard bit** is lying down and getting up again! **Be very careful!**

What about breaking blocks?

Make sure the blocks are made of **crumbly stone**. This will soak up the force from the hammer.

Crazy and not so crazy

Crazy eating

Takeru Kobayashi just loves eating; in fact, he is the eating champ (or **chump**) of the World! Takeru was born with an unusual stomach. This helps him **stuff down** huge amounts of food.

His most disgusting feat was in 2002, when he ate over 8 kilos of cow's brains in ten minutes!

In 2006 he beat the **world hot dog eating record**, eating 53 hot dogs in 12 minutes.

Michael Lotito is known a **Monsieur Mangetout**, which is French for Mr Eat Everything!

Monsieur Mangetout has eaten bicycles, TV sets and shopping trolleys. Between 1978 and 1980 **he ate an entire aeroplane**.

Human Birdmen

People have always wanted to **fly like birds**. Until 2008, every year in Bognor, England, bird-men tried to fly by jumping off the pier.

No one has managed it yet!

This picture shows the German birdman **Otto Lilienthal** in 1896.

It looks like a crazy stunt. But Otto's work was used to design hang gliders and even aircraft.

17

Feat
of
Endurance

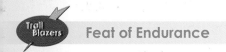

Chapter 1:
Alone

The first thing that hit Ron was the heat. Within seconds his clothes were damp with sweat.

Ron moved deeper into the rainforest, following a small stream. The noises got louder.

Woods and forests at home were quiet places. Here in the rainforest it was as noisy as a big city. There was the buzz of insects, the screaming of birds high overhead, the call of monkeys. At least, Ron guessed they were monkeys.

Ron was used to a big city. Streets full of shops and coffee bars, with people all around.

Here, Ron was alone. The boat had gone. Ron had been dumped on to the edge of a great river. He had the clothes he was wearing, and not much else.

Somehow, he had to survive.

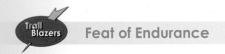
Chapter 2:
Hungry!

Ron sat down on a rock and checked through his pockets. Matches. They would be useful. A knife. A bar of chocolate that was already melting. There was no point in keeping that, so he ate it.

There was a crashing in the forest, getting closer and closer. Ron knew there weren't many dangerous large animals in the rainforest. But, just in case, he broke off a branch and sharpened the end.

Now he had a spear!

Water wasn't going to be a problem if he kept close to the stream. But what about food? There was fruit in the forest, but it might be poisonous.

Through the trees he saw a flock of parrots eating bright yellow fruit. It didn't poison them, so Ron ate it.

But fruit doesn't fill you up. He still felt hungry.

Chapter 3:
The rainforest at night

Ron thought lighting a fire would be easy. It wasn't. Everything was damp. It took half of his matches to get a fire going.

He was really hungry now.

Ron got up to put more wood on the fire. He felt something moving under his foot. Then he felt a sudden pain in his ankle.

Night-time in the rainforest …
Ow! Something bit me!
It was a snake!

He looked down and found he was standing on a snake – and the snake had just bitten him!

The snake was ready to strike again. Ron grabbed his spear and stabbed at the snake. By pure luck, he managed to kill it.

But was he hungry enough to eat a snake?

Chapter 4:
Poisoned!

Ron chopped up the snake and cooked it on a stick, like a kebab. It didn't taste *bad* – it was much, much worse than bad.

Then Ron noticed his leg was swelling up. Poison! He began to feel dizzy. His heart started to pound.

Suddenly, there was a bright light, and a face was looking down at him.

Ron lay back in the hospital bed. The producer of the 'Feat of Endurance' reality TV show was there.

"I failed, didn't I?" said Ron.

"No you didn't! You're alive Ron, so you did better than the other contestants! In a couple of days you'll be ready for your next . . . **Feat of Endurance**!"

Two days later, Ron was shivering at the North Pole. All he had was a knife and a box of matches.

Fantastic feats word check

amputated

challenge

deadlift

death zone

endurance

firewalking

frost bite

hang glider

Husafell stone

insulate

oxygen

poison

stomach

stunt

survive

tight rope

ultimate